The Rise of Darkness

Sagor sarker

Published by Sagor Sarker, 2024.

This is a work of fiction. Similarities to real people, places, or events are entirely coincidental.

THE RISE OF DARKNESS

First edition. October 28, 2024.

ISBN: 979-8227411624

Written by Sagor sarker.

Also by Sagor sarker

The Poetry of Lover's Heart
The Rise of Darkness
Love in Quiet Tremors
The Last Breath of a Love
Embrace Of Sweet Tomorrows
A Smile of Betrayal- A Novel

Watch for more at https://www.facebook.com/sagor.sarker.334/.

Table of Contents

The Rise of Darkness

Rafiqul Rahman, an eleven-year-old boy living a hard life with his strict aunt and uncle in a small village, receives a magical letter delivered by a crow on his birthday. The letter invites him to attend Afsaruddin's Magical School, a secret institution where students learn the ancient arts of magic. Intrigued and hopeful for a life beyond chores and neglect, Rafiqul follows a magical map to the mysterious Sundarbans forest, where he meets Harina, a talking deer who guides him to the school.The story explores themes of self-discovery, courage, belonging, and the moral implications of power. It weaves Bengali folklore and magic with Rafiqul's journey from being a neglected child to discovering his place in a world of wonder and danger.

Chapter 1: A Letter from the Jungle

Rafiqul leaned against the rough wall of his uncle's mud-walled house, clutching the broom tightly in his hand. The sweltering heat of midday pressed down upon the small village, and the sweat dripped from his forehead as he swept the courtyard for the third time that day. His aunt's voice screeched from inside.

"Rafiqul! What's taking so long? Are you planning to spend the whole day sweeping dust?"

"Almost done, Auntie," Rafiqul replied, his voice tinged with weariness.

He was used to this—constant chores, the cold stares from his aunt Jahanara, and the sneering comments from his cousin Fariha. His uncle

Karim rarely spoke to him except to assign more tasks or reprimand him. For as long as he could remember, Rafiqul had lived in this small house, treated more like a servant than a member of the family. He wasn't allowed to play with the other children or even attend the village school. Today, however, was different. Today was his 11th birthday, though no one in the house seemed to remember.

As he finished sweeping and moved to put the broom away, something caught his eye. A large black crow had appeared, perched on the windowsill. It was an odd sight; the bird seemed to be staring directly at him with an unsettling intensity. Before Rafiqul could shoo it away, the crow dropped a rolled parchment, tied with a red ribbon and sealed with dark wax, onto the windowsill.

He stepped closer, curiosity overcoming his caution. The seal on the parchment was marked with a strange emblem—what looked like a tiger's paw print. Rafiqul glanced around to see if anyone was watching and then quickly grabbed the letter.

The parchment felt ancient, and the seal broke easily in his hands as he unrolled it. The letters on the page seemed to shimmer and shift, written in a flowing script unlike anything he had seen before. With trembling hands, Rafiqul read aloud:

"To Rafiqul Raman, the boy who sleeps under the thatched roof,

You are hereby invited to join Afsaruddin's Magical School, where you shall learn the ancient arts of magic and sorcery. Your journey begins today. Follow the map enclosed, and do not be afraid when the path seems to disappear. Trust the magic within you."

For a moment, Rafiqul stood frozen. Magic? A magical school? It sounded like the stories he had overheard in the village—tales of old that people spoke of in hushed voices. But could it be real? And if so, why would they want someone like him? He looked inside the letter and saw a piece of parchment folded within, revealing a map that was unlike any map he had ever seen.

The lines on the map seemed to twist and turn as if alive, forming pathways that shifted and transformed. There was no doubt about it—the map pointed towards the Sundarbans, the great mangrove forest that lay beyond the village. His pulse quickened. There was a strange sense of calling, a whispering voice in the back of his mind that urged him to go.

Without waiting for a second thought, Rafiqul stuffed the letter into his pocket. He turned and ran, slipping out of the courtyard and making his way towards the edge of the village.

Chapter 2: The Path of Leaves

The edge of the Sundarbans looked like a living wall of green, the dense foliage obscuring the forest's mysteries from view. Rafiqul hesitated for a moment at the threshold. He had never ventured this far from the village alone. Stories of spirits and creatures lurking within the ancient forest haunted his thoughts. But the letter... there was something about it that seemed to pull him forward.

He took a deep breath and followed the path indicated on the map. As he walked, the trees seemed to grow thicker and closer together, their branches intertwining overhead to form a natural tunnel. The air grew cooler, and a light mist curled around the roots of the trees, carrying with it a faint, sweet fragrance. Suddenly, Rafiqul noticed something unusual: the ground beneath his feet was covered in a carpet of leaves that glowed faintly in the dim light.

The leaves appeared to move, forming a trail that led deeper into the forest. Rafiqul felt a mix of excitement and fear as he followed them. Every step seemed to echo in the quiet, as if the forest was listening.

"Rafiqul..." a voice whispered softly. He stopped, his heart racing. The voice seemed to come from everywhere and nowhere at once.

"Who's there?" Rafiqul called out, his voice shaking.

From behind a large tree stepped a deer, but not an ordinary one. This deer had antlers adorned with small glowing orbs that flickered like fireflies. Its eyes shone with intelligence, and as it approached, Rafiqul felt calmness wash over him.

"You are headed to the school, aren't you?" the deer spoke, its voice soft yet resonant. "The journey can be dangerous for one who does not know the way."

"I... I think so," Rafiqul replied, still bewildered. "Are you real? How can a deer talk?"

The deer gave a small, gentle laugh. "In this forest, many things are possible that you might not find in your everyday life. I am Harina, a guardian of this path. Come, I shall guide you."

Rafiqul followed Harina as the glowing leaves continued to guide their way. The trees seemed to move aside for them, and Rafiqul noticed glimpses of strange creatures in the shadows—glowing eyes, whispers of wings, the rustling of unseen beings.

As they went deeper, the forest seemed to hum with an ancient power, as though it recognized Rafiqul and welcomed him. The map in his pocket grew warm, as if it was alive, and Rafiqul began to realize that the world he had known was only a small part of something much larger, much more wondrous.

Chapter 3: Afsaruddin's Magical School

After what seemed like hours, they reached a clearing. At the center stood a towering structure, part temple, part ancient tree, with roots that seemed to grow into the very walls. The school appeared to be alive, entwined with vines and flowers that bloomed with an unnatural light. The air was filled with the sound of distant bells, and Rafiqul could see other children his age, some floating on enchanted carpets, others practicing spells with glowing staffs.

"Welcome to Afsaruddin's Magical School," Harina said, bowing its head. "This is where you will begin your new life, Rafiqul. But remember, the magic here is as deep as the roots of these ancient trees, and there are dangers as well as wonders."

Rafiqul could hardly believe his eyes. The place was like nothing he had ever imagined, filled with enchantments and secrets waiting to be discovered. And for the first time, a feeling of belonging stirred within him.

Chapter 4: The Headmaster's Welcome

Rafiqul stood at the entrance of the school, awestruck by the sight before him. The building seemed to breathe with magic, its walls covered in ancient carvings that glowed with a faint blue light. Above, a large dome made of intertwined branches and leaves let in shafts of sunlight, creating a mosaic of light and shadow on the ground. Students moved around the courtyard, some wearing robes of deep green and gold, others practicing with staffs that glowed like the moon.

Harina, the talking deer, led him towards a set of wooden doors. "Go inside, Rafiqul. The headmaster has been expecting you," it said before disappearing into the forest without another word.

Rafiqul hesitated for a moment, then took a deep breath and pushed open the doors. He found himself in a large hall with walls lined with bookshelves that stretched up to the ceiling. The air smelled of old parchment and something sweet, like freshly ground spices. At the far end of the hall sat an old man with a long, flowing beard and twinkling eyes. He wore a robe that seemed to shimmer like water under moonlight, and a hat shaped like a cobra's hood.

"Ah, Rafiqul Rahman! Welcome to Afsaruddin's Magical School," the old man said warmly, his voice deep and kind. "I am Headmaster Kuddus Afsaruddin. Please, come closer."

Rafiqul approached cautiously, still overwhelmed by everything that had happened. "You—you knew I was coming?" he asked, feeling a little embarrassed by the question.

"Of course," Headmaster Afsaruddin replied with a chuckle. "This school has existed for hundreds of years, hidden from the eyes of ordinary people, and I can sense when a new student is on the path. We have been watching you for some time, Rafiqul. There is a special magic inside you that must be nurtured. That is why you are here."

"Magic?" Rafiqul echoed. "But I don't know anything about magic. I didn't even know it was real until today."

"Magic is real, indeed," the headmaster said, leaning forward with a serious expression. "But it is not just about spells and enchantments. It is about understanding the forces of nature, the spirits that reside in the world, and the secrets hidden within our own hearts. You will learn all these things here, and more."

He waved his hand, and a staff appeared in midair, floating towards Rafiqul. The staff was made of polished wood, with a carved tiger's head at the top and symbols etched along its length.

"This is your 'Bongshoboti,' a staff that will help you channel your magic," said the headmaster. "Each student receives one when they first arrive, and the staff chooses its master. Try holding it, and see how it feels."

Rafiqul reached out and grasped the staff. A sudden warmth spread through his hand, and he felt a strange but comforting tingle run up his arm. It was as if the staff was alive and welcoming him.

"Very good," the headmaster said, nodding approvingly. "Now, there are a few rules that you must remember. The first is that you must never use magic to harm another person unless it is in self-defense. The second is that you must respect the spirits and creatures of the forest; they are our allies and our guides. And finally, you must always trust your own heart. It will lead you when nothing else can."

Rafiqul nodded, feeling both excited and nervous. There was so much to learn, and he wasn't sure if he was ready.

"Do not worry," the headmaster said, as if reading his thoughts. "You will learn in time, just as every other student here has. Now, go and join your fellow students. Classes will begin soon, and you will have much to discover."

Chapter 5: The First Lesson

Rafiqul wandered out of the headmaster's hall and found himself in a large open courtyard surrounded by classrooms. Other students his age were already gathered there, and many of them seemed to know each other. Feeling a bit out of place, he looked around until he noticed a boy with untidy hair and a mischievous grin practicing with his staff.

"Hey, are you new here too?" the boy called out to him.

"Yes," Rafiqul replied, walking over. "I'm Rafiqul. I just arrived today."

"I'm Aslam," the boy said, shaking Rafiqul's hand enthusiastically. "Nice to meet you! This place is amazing, isn't it? My parents used to tell me stories about it, but I never thought it would be this... magical!"

Rafiqul couldn't help but smile at Aslam's excitement. It was nice to find someone else who seemed just as overwhelmed as he was.

Their first class was held in a room with walls made entirely of living branches and leaves. Sunlight streamed through the gaps, and the scent of fresh earth filled the air. Professor Nuri, a tall woman with silver hair and deep-set eyes, stood at the front, her "Bongshoboti" staff resting against the wall.

"Welcome, new students," she began, her voice calm yet commanding. "Today, we will learn the basics of magic—how to focus your energy and channel it through your staff. Magic comes from the world around you, but it is guided by your will. Concentrate on your staff and feel the energy flow through it."

Rafiqul closed his eyes and held his staff tightly; trying to sense the energy Professor Nuri spoke of. At first, there was nothing. Just silence and the sound of the wind. Then, slowly, he began to feel a warmth in his hand, spreading up his arm and through his chest. It was faint, like a flickering flame, but it was there.

He opened his eyes and saw that the symbols on his staff were glowing. A small orb of light appeared at the tip, pulsing gently.

"Very good, Rafiqul," Professor Nuri said, nodding approvingly. "You have a natural connection to magic. With practice, you will be able to control it better."

Rafiqul felt a rush of excitement and relief. He could actually do magic! It wasn't just a dream or a trick. He glanced over at Aslam, who was still struggling to get his staff to glow. Aslam caught his eye and grinned sheepishly.

"Looks like you're a natural," he said. "I'm still trying to figure out which end of this thing is supposed to light up."

Rafiqul chuckled, feeling more at ease. For the first time, he felt like he belonged somewhere, and the thought filled him with a sense of hope he had never known before.

Chapter 6: The Mystery of the Old Library

After their first day of lessons, Rafiqul and Aslam wandered around the school, exploring its many corridors and hidden passages. There was a sense of endless discovery in the air, as if every corner held a secret waiting to be uncovered.

They came upon an old library, its entrance marked by an archway of twisted roots. Unlike the other parts of the school, the library seemed ancient and forgotten. Dust covered the shelves, and the books looked as though they hadn't been touched in years.

"Let's go in," Aslam said, already stepping through the archway. "I bet there's all sorts of interesting things in here."

Rafiqul followed hesitantly, glancing around. As they wandered deeper, he noticed a book on a pedestal at the center of the room. It was bound in faded leather, with symbols that glowed faintly in the dim light. When Rafiqul approached it, the book seemed to whisper, as if calling out to him.

"Hey, do you hear that?" he asked, turning to Aslam.

"Hear what?" Aslam replied, frowning. "I don't hear anything."

Rafiqul reached out to touch the book, and the moment his fingers brushed the cover, a sudden chill ran through the room. The whispers grew louder, and the symbols on the book began to pulse with a dark blue light.

"Rafiqul, I don't think we should be messing with that," Aslam said, taking a step back.

But before Rafiqul could pull his hand away, the book flew open, and a gust of wind blew through the library, scattering papers and knocking over a stack of books. The light in the room dimmed, and the whispering voices rose to a feverish pitch.

Then, as suddenly as it began, everything went silent.

Rafiqul and Aslam stared at each other, wide-eyed. The book lay open, and its pages glowed faintly. In the center was a symbol that Rafiqul did not recognize, surrounded by words written in a language he could not understand. But there was one thing that stood out—etched into the corner of the page was a dark mark shaped like a tiger's paw, just like the seal on the letter Rafiqul had received.

Chapter 7: The Hidden Mark

Rafiqul stared at the strange mark shaped like a tiger's paw. It was the same symbol that had been on the letter delivered by the crow. What did it mean? As he reached out to trace the outline of the paw print with his finger, a low rumble echoed through the room. The air seemed to grow thicker, and the pages of the book shimmered, almost as if they were made of water.

Suddenly, a shadowy figure emerged from the pages, forming a vague shape of a man cloaked in darkness. It hovered above the book, its voice low and raspy. "The mark of the shikorer," it whispered. "Beware, young sorcerer. Some paths lead only to darkness.

Before Rafiqul could react, the figure dissipated into thin air, leaving the room in silence. He turned to Aslam, who had backed away several steps and looked as though he had seen a ghost.

"What was that?" Aslam asked, his voice shaking. "And what's a shikorer?"

"I don't know," Rafiqul replied, his mind racing. "But I think it's connected to the letter I received, and maybe even to why I was invited here. The mark was the same, Aslam."

Aslam's eyes widened. "Do you think the headmaster knows about this? Should we tell him?"

Rafiqul hesitated. "No, not yet," he said finally. "I need to understand more about this symbol first. If it's important, there must be something in the library that explains it."

The boys spent the next hour searching the library for any mention of the shikorer, the tiger's paw mark, or anything similar. But most of the books were written in languages they couldn't understand, and the few they could read mentioned nothing about the symbol. It was as if the library had been hiding its secrets from them.

As they were about to give up, Aslam stumbled upon a narrow, dust-covered book tucked behind a row of old scrolls. The cover was plain, but the title was faintly visible: *"The Forgotten Legends of Bengal's Magic."*

"Look at this!" Aslam said, handing the book to Rafiqul. "This might have something about that symbol."

Rafiqul quickly flipped through the pages, scanning the text for any mention of the shikorer. After a few moments, he found a passage that caught his attention:

"The Shikorer, or 'The Rooted Ones,' were a group of powerful sorcerers said to have wielded magic drawn from the ancient spirits of the forest. Their symbol was the paw of a tiger, which represented their bond with the spirits and the secrets hidden deep within the Sundarbans. It is said that their knowledge came at a price, for the magic they practiced could blur the line between the light and the dark."

Rafiqul's heart raced. This was no coincidence. There was a connection between the tiger's paw and whatever magic was calling to him. But what was the price that the book spoke of? And why was the mark appearing now?

"I think this has something to do with me," Rafiqul said quietly. "I need to find out more about the Shikorer and their magic. Maybe that's why I was invited here—to uncover a secret that's been hidden for years."

Chapter 8: The Trials of the Forest

The next day, Rafiqul and Aslam returned to their lessons, but the encounter in the library lingered in Rafiqul's mind. He could not shake the feeling that the mysterious figure's warning had been meant for him, and he began to notice strange things happening around the school. Sometimes, when he was practicing with his staff, shadows would flicker at the edges of his vision. Other times, the symbols on his staff glowed faintly even when he wasn't trying to cast a spell.

One afternoon, during a lesson on summoning protective charms, Professor Nuri announced a special task for the new students. "Today, we will begin the Trials of the Forest," she said. "This is a tradition for all first-year students, meant to test your courage, your magic, and your understanding of the forest's spirits. You will be given a task that requires you to retrieve an item from the depths of the Sundarbans. But beware; the forest will not make your journey easy."

The students buzzed with excitement and nervous whispers. The Trials were known to be challenging, and many older students had spoken of the strange things they had encountered during their tasks.

"You will go in pairs," Professor Nuri continued, "and each pair will be assigned a specific item to retrieve. The magic of the forest will guide you if you listen carefully."

Rafiqul and Aslam were paired together and assigned to find a "Bhootful," a rare flower said to bloom only in the darkest parts of the forest. It was said to glow with a pale blue light and to possess strong magical properties.

The boys set out towards the forest, their staffs in hand. As they ventured deeper, the trees seemed to close in around them, their roots twisting like the limbs of sleeping giants. The light grew dim, and a faint mist hung in the air. Rafiqul could feel the magic of the place pressing against his skin, like a pulse beneath the earth.

"Do you think the Bhootful will be easy to find?" Aslam asked, glancing around nervously.

"Probably not," Rafiqul replied, tightening his grip on his staff. "But the headmaster said we should trust our instincts. I think we need to let the magic guide us."

As they moved further into the forest, the mist thickened, and strange sounds began to echo around them—whispers that seemed to come from the shadows, and the rustling of leaves with no wind to move them. Rafiqul felt the hairs on the back of his neck stand up. It was as if the forest itself was watching them.

"Rafiqul, look!" Aslam suddenly pointed ahead. Through the mist, they saw a faint blue glow, flickering like the flame of a distant lantern.

They cautiously made their way towards the light, and soon they saw it—a Bhootful, glowing softly in the darkness, its petals like silk. But as Rafiqul reached out to pluck the flower, a deep growl rumbled from the shadows.

Emerging from the darkness was a massive creature, its eyes glowing a fierce yellow. It looked like a tiger, but larger than any tiger Rafiqul had ever seen, with fur that shimmered as if made of smoke and fire.

"Back away slowly," Rafiqul whispered to Aslam, but the tiger took a step forward, baring its fangs. Rafiqul could feel a surge of magic in the air—powerful and wild, like a storm about to break.

Suddenly, the symbols on Rafiqul's staff flared with light, and the tiger paused, its gaze locking onto the staff. It growled again, but this time, there was something different in its eyes—a recognition.

Rafiqul took a deep breath and raised his staff, willing the magic to come to him. "We're not here to harm you," he said, his voice steady. "We only need the flower."

The tiger let out a low rumble, then slowly backed away into the shadows, as if conceding. Rafiqul quickly plucked the Bhootful and the boys hurried out of the forest, their hearts racing.

Chapter 9: The Headmaster's Revelation

When they returned to the school with the Bhootful, Professor Nuri seemed impressed, but Rafiqul couldn't shake the feeling that there was more to the encounter with the tiger than he understood. That evening, he went to see Headmaster Afsaruddin.

The headmaster listened carefully as Rafiqul described what had happened in the forest. When Rafiqul finished, the headmaster sat back in his chair, his expression thoughtful.

"The tiger you saw was not an ordinary creature," the headmaster said slowly. "It was a guardian spirit of the Sundarbans, one that has watched over these lands for centuries. It recognized something in you, Rafiqul—a connection to the magic of the Shikorer."

"But what does that mean?" Rafiqul asked, his voice filled with uncertainty.

"It means, young sorcerer, that your path is entwined with the old magic—magic that is powerful, but not without its dangers," the headmaster replied. "The Shikorer were known for walking the line between light and darkness. There is much you still need to learn, and it may not be an easy journey. But you have the potential to unlock secrets that have been lost for ages."

Rafiqul's mind swirled with questions, but he knew one thing for certain: the mark of the Shikorer was not just a symbol. It was a part of him. And whatever secrets it held, he was determined to uncover them.

Chapter 10: The Symbol's Legacy

The headmaster's words weighed heavily on Rafiqul's mind as he left the office that evening. The idea that he had a connection to an ancient and potentially dangerous magic made him uneasy. But it also sparked a determination within him—he needed to learn more about the Shikorer and why their mark kept appearing in his life.

The next day, Rafiqul shared the headmaster's revelation with Aslam, who listened intently. "So, the tiger was some kind of guardian spirit?" Aslam said, his voice filled with wonder. "That's incredible! But it sounds like there's a lot more we don't know. How do we find out what it all means?"

"I think we need to keep looking in the library," Rafiqul replied. "There has to be more information about the Shikorer hidden somewhere in those old books. If the headmaster knows more, he's not telling me yet."

The boys returned to the library later that night, sneaking in quietly so as not to attract attention. They went back to the narrow book they had found earlier, *The Forgotten Legends of Bengal's Magic,* and began searching for more references to the Shikorer.

Rafiqul soon found a passage that described the origins of the group. "Listen to this," he said, his voice hushed with excitement. "It says, 'The Shikorer were formed in a time of great turmoil, when dark forces threatened to consume the magic of Bengal. The sorcerers who became the Shikorer sought to preserve the balance between light and shadow, drawing on the power of the forest itself to bind evil spirits and keep them from spreading chaos.'"

"That explains why the tiger seemed to recognize your staff," Aslam said. "Maybe it sensed that you have the same kind of magic they used."

Rafiqul nodded thoughtfully. "But why did it appear now? What if the evil spirits the Shikorer fought against are returning? What if that's why the mark keeps showing up?"

Just as he spoke, a low creaking noise echoed through the library. The boys froze, turning towards the source of the sound. The old wooden doors of the library were slowly swinging open, and a shadowy figure stood in the doorway.

It was Professor Nuri.

"What are you two doing in here so late?" she asked, her voice calm but stern. "The library is off-limits at night."

Rafiqul and Aslam exchanged nervous glances. "We were... um, doing some extra reading," Rafiqul said quickly. "We found something about the Shikorer and wanted to learn more."

Professor Nuri's eyes narrowed. "The Shikorer, you say?" She took a step closer, her expression softening slightly. "That is an unusual topic for a pair of first-year students. Come with me. There is something you need to see."

Chapter 11: The Secret Chamber

Professor Nuri led Rafiqul and Aslam down a narrow corridor lined with old portraits, their painted eyes seeming to follow the boys as they walked. At the end of the corridor was a door that looked different from the others—its surface was carved with intricate symbols and runes, some of which glowed faintly as Professor Nuri approached.

She whispered a few words under her breath, and the symbols on the door shimmered before fading away. With a gentle push, she opened the door, revealing a spiral staircase leading downward. "Follow me," she said, starting down the steps.

The boys hesitated for a moment before following her. The staircase seemed to descend forever, and the air grew cooler the further they went. Eventually, they emerged into a large underground chamber lit by dozens of floating orbs of blue light. The walls were covered in ancient tapestries and carvings, many of which featured the tiger's paw symbol.

In the center of the room stood a stone pedestal, and on top of it lay an old, leather-bound book. Professor Nuri walked over to the pedestal and placed her hand on the book. "This is the *Chronicle of the Shikorer,*" she said. "It is one of the few remaining records of the group's history and magic. Very few people have access to this knowledge, but if you are indeed connected to their legacy, then you should see it."

She opened the book to a page near the middle, where a detailed illustration showed a group of sorcerers standing in a circle around a massive tiger. The text described a ritual known as *Bondhon,* which was used by the Shikorer to seal away dark spirits. It required channeling magic through a special artifact known as the *Shikor-Botol,* or the "Root Vessel," which could contain and bind even the most malevolent forces.

Rafiqul's gaze lingered on the image of the tiger. "Professor, why are we learning about this now?" he asked. "Is there something dangerous happening that we need to know about?"

Professor Nuri took a deep breath before replying. "There have been signs," she said quietly. "Disturbances in the forest, whispers of shadows moving in places where they shouldn't. The headmaster and I have been monitoring the situation, but we don't know the full extent of what's happening. If there is a threat, it may be connected to the Shikorer's old enemies."

Rafiqul felt a chill run down his spine. "What do we need to do?" he asked, his voice steady despite the unease building inside him.

"You must continue your studies and prepare yourselves," Professor Nuri replied. "There may come a time when you will need to use what you have learned to protect the school and the forest. I will help you as much as I can, but the path ahead is uncertain. The magic you possess is powerful, Rafiqul, but it can also be dangerous if not controlled."

She handed him the *Chronicle of the Shikorer*. "Take this. Study it, but be cautious. Some knowledge is meant to be kept hidden for a reason."

Chapter 12: The Return of the Shadows

Over the following weeks, Rafiqul and Aslam dedicated themselves to learning as much as they could about the Shikorer. They studied the spells in the *Chronicle*, practiced rituals, and learned about the protective charms that had once been used to guard against dark spirits. Rafiqul's connection to his staff seemed to grow stronger with each passing day, and he could feel the magic flowing through him more naturally.

However, strange occurrences continued to plague the school. Students reported seeing shadowy figures at the edge of the forest, and some even claimed to hear whispers in a language they didn't recognize. It was as if something was lurking just out of sight, waiting for the right moment to strike.

One night, as Rafiqul lay in bed, he was awoken by a sudden chill. The air around him seemed to grow heavy, and he felt a familiar presence—like the one he had encountered in the old library. He sat up and saw a faint shadow moving outside his window, slipping into the darkness of the forest.

Without thinking, Rafiqul grabbed his staff and hurried outside. The moonlight cast long, eerie shadows on the ground, and the night was silent except for the distant rustling of leaves. He followed the shadow's trail, his heart pounding.

As he reached the edge of the forest, he saw it—a figure cloaked in darkness, standing under a large tree. Its eyes glowed a deep red, and when it spoke, its voice was like a hiss.

"You are one of them," the figure said. "A descendant of the Shikorer. You should not have meddled with the old magic, boy."

Rafiqul raised his staff, the symbols on it glowing brightly. "Who are you? What do you want?" he demanded.

The figure's laughter was like a cold wind. "What I want is beyond your understanding, little sorcerer. But you... you and your kind will not stand in my way again."

Before Rafiqul could react, the figure lunged at him, moving with unnatural speed. He instinctively raised his staff, and a bright flash of light erupted from it, pushing the shadowy figure back. The creature hissed and vanished into the darkness, leaving behind only a lingering chill in the air.

Breathing heavily, Rafiqul looked down at his staff. The symbols continued to glow faintly, as if still resonating with the magic he had just unleashed. He knew that this was only the beginning. Whatever was out there was growing stronger, and he needed to be ready.

The Shikorer's legacy had returned, and Rafiqul was about to find out just how deep its roots went.

Chapter 13: The Gathering Storm

The next morning, Rafiqul told Aslam about the encounter with the shadowy figure in the forest. Aslam's face paled when he heard about the creature's red eyes and the cold laughter.

"This is getting serious," Aslam said. "If dark spirits are starting to appear, we need to tell the headmaster or Professor Nuri. We can't handle this on our own!"

Rafiqul hesitated. He felt the weight of what the figure had said—that he was "one of them," a descendant of the Shikorer. If the darkness was returning, then it seemed like it was tied to him in some way. "Not yet," he said, shaking his head. "If we go to the headmaster now, they might not let us investigate further. We need to find out more on our own first."

Aslam reluctantly agreed, though the worry didn't leave his face. "Fine. But if things get any worse, we have to tell them. Promise me."

"I promise," Rafiqul said, though he wasn't sure if he could keep that promise. His thoughts kept returning to the Chronicle of the Shikorer. There was a ritual mentioned near the back of the book called *Shikorbondhon*—a binding spell used by the Shikorer to trap dark spirits and seal away evil. It required an artifact known as the *Dhrubo-Shikor,* a powerful charm said to contain the essence of the forest's magic.

The boys spent the next few days searching the library and consulting old scrolls, trying to find any clues about the Dhrubo-Shikor. Eventually, they found a reference to it in a dusty old manuscript that described a hidden shrine deep within the Sundarbans, where the charm was supposedly kept.

"If we find the Dhrubo-Shikor," Rafiqul said, his voice filled with determination, "we might be able to use the binding ritual to seal away whatever is causing these disturbances."

"But the shrine could be anywhere in the Sundarbans," Aslam pointed out. "We can't search the whole forest! And even if we do find it, there's no guarantee the charm is still there."

Rafiqul glanced at his staff. "I think the staff might help us find it. Whenever we're near powerful magic, the symbols glow, right? Maybe it can lead us to the shrine."

The plan was risky, but they didn't have any better options. The boys decided to head into the forest the following night, under the cover of darkness.

Chapter 14: Into the Heart of the Forest

The night of the search was clear and still, the moon casting silver light over the trees. Rafiqul and Aslam crept out of the school grounds and made their way into the forest. As they ventured deeper, Rafiqul felt a familiar tingling sensation in his fingertips, and the symbols on his staff began to glow faintly.

The further they went, the more the air seemed to thicken with magic. The leaves rustled in strange patterns, and whispers drifted on the breeze, sounding almost like words. After what felt like hours of walking, they reached a part of the forest that seemed different—older, more ancient. The trees here were larger, their roots gnarled and twisted, and the mist was thicker than anywhere else they had been.

"There's something here," Rafiqul said, his voice barely above a whisper. He felt drawn towards a large tree with a hollow at its base. The opening was wide enough for them to crawl through, and inside, a dim blue light flickered.

Aslam peered inside and saw that the hollow led to a narrow tunnel descending into the earth. "Do you think this is it?" he asked.

Rafiqul nodded. "It has to be."

They squeezed through the opening and began their descent, using Rafiqul's glowing staff to light the way. The tunnel spiraled downward, and the air grew colder as they went deeper. After several minutes, the passage opened into a wide chamber. In the center stood an altar made of stone, and resting atop it was a small wooden box carved with symbols similar to those on Rafiqul's staff.

"This must be the Dhrubo-Shikor," Rafiqul said, his voice echoing in the chamber. He reached out to open the box, but just as his fingers touched the wood, a cold wind swept through the room, and the shadows seemed to shift and swirl around them.

From the darkness emerged a figure—a tall, cloaked shape with eyes that burned like red coals. It was the same creature that had confronted Rafiqul outside the school.

"You should not have come here," it said, its voice filled with malice. "The Dhrubo-Shikor belongs to me now, and no descendant of the Shikorer will take it away."

Rafiqul gripped his staff tightly. "We're not leaving without it," he said defiantly. "You can't stop us."

The figure laughed, a chilling sound that echoed off the stone walls. "Foolish boy. You know nothing of the forces you meddle with. The Shikorer could not defeat me before, and you are nothing compared to them."

It lunged towards them, and Rafiqul raised his staff, calling upon the magic of the forest. The symbols glowed brightly, and a burst of light erupted from the staff, pushing the creature back. Aslam quickly grabbed the box from the altar and held it close.

"Run!" Rafiqul shouted.

The boys sprinted back towards the tunnel, with the shadowy figure in pursuit. It moved swiftly, closing the distance between them, but Rafiqul and Aslam kept running, fueled by fear and determination. When they reached the entrance to the hollow, they scrambled out and slammed their backs against the tree, gasping for breath.

The figure did not emerge from the hollow. It was as if the forest itself had sealed the entrance behind them.

"We need to get back to the school," Aslam said, his voice trembling. "And tell the headmaster everything."

Rafiqul agreed. There was no longer any doubt in his mind that the danger was real and growing. The darkness was returning, and they would need all the help they could get to stop it.

Chapter 15: Unveiling the Truth

The boys returned to the school in the dead of night, sneaking back into the dormitories without being seen. As soon as morning came, they went straight to Headmaster Afsaruddin's office, bringing the Dhrubo-Shikor with them.

The headmaster listened intently as they recounted their journey into the forest, the discovery of the hidden chamber, and the encounter with the shadowy figure. When they showed him the wooden box containing the Dhrubo-Shikor, his expression grew somber.

"You have done well to bring this back," he said, opening the box to reveal a small crystal orb nestled within. The orb shimmered with a pale blue light, and strange symbols seemed to swirl within its depths. "This is indeed the Dhrubo-Shikor, a powerful charm that was used by the Shikorer to bind evil spirits. It is an artifact of great significance, and it may be the key to sealing away whatever dark force has been awakened."

Rafiqul felt a surge of relief, but also a sense of responsibility. "What is the shadowy figure we saw?" he asked. "It said the Shikorer couldn't defeat it before."

The headmaster's eyes darkened. "It is a spirit of great malice known as *Kaal-Nishachor*—a being that feeds on fear and thrives in the darkness. Long ago, the Shikorer tried to bind it using the Dhrubo-Shikor, but they could only weaken it, not destroy it completely. For many years, it was kept at bay, but something has allowed it to grow stronger again."

Rafiqul and Aslam exchanged a worried glance. "How do we stop it?" Rafiqul asked.

"You will need to perform the *Shikorbondhon* ritual," the headmaster said. "But it will not be easy. The binding spell requires great focus and strength, and Kaal-Nishachor will not go down without a fight. You must prepare yourselves, for this will be a test unlike any you have faced before."

The boys nodded, determination burning in their eyes. The time had come to face the darkness head-on and embrace the legacy of the Shikorer. They had to succeed—because if they failed, the entire school, and perhaps all of Bengal, would fall under the shadow of Kaal-Nishachor.

Chapter 16: The Dark Pact

With the Dhrubo-Shikor in their possession, Rafiqul and Aslam felt a surge of hope, but the gravity of what lay ahead weighed heavily on their minds. The headmaster insisted on keeping the ritual preparations secret, fearing that the panic among the students could empower Kaal-Nishachor even more.

As the days passed, Rafiqul and Aslam trained tirelessly under Professor Nuri's guidance, practicing complex incantations and perfecting their control over the forest's magic. The professor taught them a variety of ancient techniques used by the Shikorer—how to manipulate roots to form barriers, summon protective animals, and focus their energy into the Dhrubo-Shikor for the binding ritual. Yet, even as they made progress, an uneasiness crept in. Kaal-Nishachor seemed to be growing bolder. Disturbing visions plagued Rafiqul's sleep, images of shadowy figures surrounding the school, whispering his name, beckoning him to join the darkness.

One night, as he lay in bed struggling to fall asleep, a sudden pull in his chest stirred him awake. His staff, resting by the bed, was glowing faintly. Rafiqul felt an urge—a strange compulsion—drawing him towards the forest. He grabbed the staff, threw on his cloak, and quietly left the dormitory.

He walked in a daze, following the feeling that guided him deeper and deeper into the woods. The air was heavy, and the familiar chill of Kaal-Nishachor's presence loomed around him. As Rafiqul stepped into a moonlit clearing, he saw a figure standing at the center—a dark silhouette with glowing red eyes.

"You've finally come," Kaal-Nishachor said, its voice dripping with malice. "I knew you wouldn't resist."

Rafiqul gripped his staff, keeping his fear at bay. "What do you want?" he demanded. "Why do you keep coming for me?"

Kaal-Nishachor's laughter sent shivers down his spine. "I come for you because you are more like me than you think," it whispered. "The Shikorer believed they could control the darkness, but they never understood its true power. You, however... you could become so much more."

The figure raised its hands, and shadows swirled around Rafiqul like a living storm. "Join me," it hissed. "Embrace the darkness, and I will show you secrets beyond your wildest imagination. The magic you wield now is nothing compared to the power I can give you."

For a moment, Rafiqul felt an overwhelming temptation. The shadows felt oddly comforting, as if they were offering him freedom, strength beyond measure. But then he remembered Aslam's face, the headmaster's stern warnings, and the Shikorer's duty to protect the balance of magic. He couldn't betray them.

"No!" Rafiqul shouted, lifting his staff high as it erupted with brilliant light. The burst of magic pushed Kaal-Nishachor back, dispelling the shadows momentarily.

"You will regret this choice, boy," the dark spirit growled, its form shifting and dissolving back into the night. "The time will come when you will wish you had listened."

Rafiqul stood trembling in the clearing, his heart racing. He knew the danger was greater than he had imagined. Kaal-Nishachor's words echoed in his mind, but he pushed them aside. He was more determined than ever to seal the darkness away once and for all.

Chapter 17: The Forgotten Ally

The next morning, Rafiqul shared the encounter with Aslam and Professor Nuri. Aslam's worry deepened, and Professor Nuri's expression was grim.

"It seems that Kaal-Nishachor is trying to weaken your resolve," Professor Nuri said. "You must not let its words poison your mind, Rafiqul. But there is something else I haven't told you, something that might help."

She led them back to the secret chamber below the school, where the *Chronicle of the Shikorer* lay open on the pedestal. She turned to a section near the end, showing a detailed illustration of a mystical beast—a white tiger with golden eyes.

"This is *Aranyan*, a legendary guardian of the forest," she said. "The Shikorer called upon it in times of great need to aid them in their battles against dark forces. It is said that the tiger sleeps within the heart of the forest and can only be awakened by a sorcerer of true courage."

Rafiqul's eyes widened with realization. "Could Aranyan help us bind Kaal-Nishachor?" he asked.

Professor Nuri nodded. "If you can awaken the guardian, its power will bolster the Dhrubo-Shikor during the ritual. But finding Aranyan will not be easy. The Shikorer hid the location of the shrine where the tiger rests. You will need to seek out the *Forest's Breath,* an ancient charm that can reveal hidden pathways."

Rafiqul felt a surge of hope. "Where do we find this charm?"

"It was last seen in the possession of a hermit sorcerer known as *Goriber Dadu,*" she said. "He lives in a secluded part of the Sundarbans. Be warned, he is unpredictable and not always willing to help."

Rafiqul and Aslam wasted no time. That very evening, they set out towards the part of the forest where the hermit was said to dwell. The journey was treacherous, with uneven paths and thick vegetation that seemed almost alive. They eventually stumbled upon a small hut made of mud and leaves, nestled under a massive banyan tree.

"Hello?" Rafiqul called out. "Is anyone here? We seek the Forest's Breath charm."

From the shadows emerged a frail old man with a long beard, his eyes twinkling mischievously. "The Forest's Breath, you say?" Goriber Dadu replied in a raspy voice. "Why should I give it to you, eh? Young sorcerers always meddling with things beyond their understanding."

Rafiqul took a step forward. "We need it to awaken Aranyan and stop Kaal-Nishachor," he explained. "The darkness is returning, and we don't have much time."

The old man cackled, shaking his head. "Kaal-Nishachor? You think a couple of boys can stand against that beast? What makes you worthy of the Forest's Breath?"

Rafiqul hesitated but then spoke with conviction. "Because I've already faced it, and I didn't back down. Because if we don't try, the darkness will consume everything. I can't let that happen."

For a moment, the hermit was silent, studying Rafiqul with an intense gaze. Then, with a slow nod, he turned and reached into the folds of his cloak, pulling out a small wooden amulet carved in the shape of a leaf. It glowed faintly as he handed it to Rafiqul.

"The Forest's Breath will show you the path to Aranyan's shrine," he said, his tone surprisingly serious. "But be careful, boy. Not all who seek the guardian find it, and those who fail... may never return."

Chapter 18: The Awakening

With the Forest's Breath in hand, Rafiqul and Aslam followed the charm's magic, which guided them deeper into the most ancient parts of the Sundarbans. The air was filled with a heavy mist, and strange animal calls echoed from the shadows. Yet, Rafiqul could feel the amulet's warmth in his palm, reassuring him that they were on the right path.

After hours of trekking, they finally arrived at a sacred grove. At the center lay a massive stone altar surrounded by statues of ancient sorcerers, their expressions solemn and watchful. Rafiqul placed the Dhrubo-Shikor on the altar, and as he did, the symbols on his staff began to glow once again. He knew it was time to call upon Aranyan.

He raised the Forest's Breath high, chanting an incantation from the *Chronicle of the Shikorer.* The mist thickened, swirling around the altar, and the ground trembled as if the forest itself was waking. Then, out of the mist, a massive white tiger emerged, its golden eyes gleaming with ancient wisdom.

"Aranyan..." Rafiqul whispered in awe.

The guardian tiger approached the boys, its gaze piercing yet calm. "You have summoned me, young sorcerer," it spoke, its voice echoing in the air. "Why do you call upon my power?"

Rafiqul took a deep breath, his resolve unwavering. "To bind Kaal-Nishachor and protect the forest," he said. "We need your strength to complete the ritual and seal away the darkness."

Aranyan regarded him thoughtfully before nodding. "Very well," it said. "But know this—the binding ritual will not just test your magic. It will test your spirit. You must not waver, or the darkness will claim you."

With that, the tiger lay beside the altar, its presence radiating powerful magic. Rafiqul could feel the Dhrubo-Shikor pulsing with new energy, ready for the final confrontation.

But even as the grove filled with the light of the awakened guardian, a shadow loomed on the horizon. Kaal-Nishachor was coming, and it would take everything they had to defeat it.

Chapter 19: The Gathering of Shadows

The air grew colder as dusk settled over the grove, and the atmosphere thickened with an ominous energy. Rafiqul, Aslam, and Aranyan prepared themselves for the final confrontation. The forest seemed to hold its breath, as if aware of the impending battle between light and shadow.

Kaal-Nishachor's presence became palpable—a chill that crawled under their skin, as the darkness itself seemed to stir and whisper. The sky darkened unnaturally, and from the depths of the forest, shadows began to stretch and twist, converging on the grove. With every step closer, the cold laughter of the dark spirit echoed in the air.

"It's coming," Aslam said, his voice tense. His hands tightened around his own staff, which flickered with blue flames in response to the rising threat.

Rafiqul stood at the altar with the Dhrubo-Shikor, focusing his energy on the binding ritual. He could feel the guardian tiger's presence amplifying his power. Aranyan's fur shimmered with a silver glow as it bared its fangs, a low growl rumbling in its throat.

Kaal-Nishachor finally appeared, emerging from the shadows like a figure stepping out of a nightmare. Its shape seemed fluid, shifting between human and beast, with eyes burning a deep, malevolent red. It glanced at the Dhrubo-Shikor and then at Rafiqul.

"Still playing the hero, are we?" the dark spirit sneered. "Do you think a boy and his pet can stand against the darkness itself?"

"Enough talk!" Rafiqul shouted, slamming his staff into the ground. "We're ending this, right here, right now!"

The Dhrubo-Shikor glowed with an intense blue light as Rafiqul began chanting the ancient incantation of *Shikorbondhon.* The words of the spell echoed through the grove, merging with the whispers of the forest. As he spoke, roots and vines erupted from the ground, encircling Kaal-Nishachor in an attempt to bind it.

But the dark spirit was not so easily subdued. It roared, sending a shockwave of darkness that shattered the vines and roots. "Foolish child! The Shikorer failed to seal me because they feared the darkness. You do not have the strength to overcome that fear!"

Kaal-Nishachor lashed out, sending a wave of shadow towards Rafiqul and Aslam. Aranyan sprang into action, leaping between the boys and the darkness, absorbing the attack with a growl. The tiger's eyes blazed like golden suns, pushing back the darkness with a powerful burst of light.

"Stay focused, Rafiqul!" Aranyan's voice resonated in his mind. "Do not let doubt cloud your spirit!"

Rafiqul gritted his teeth and continued the incantation, pouring all his energy into the Dhrubo-Shikor. Aslam joined in, his staff glowing brighter as he channeled his magic to support the binding spell. The combined magic created a barrier of light around the grove, trapping Kaal-Nishachor within.

But the dark spirit was not yet defeated. It snarled and began to change form once again, transforming into a colossal serpent made of shadow. The serpent lunged at them, its fangs gleaming like dark crystals. It struck at the barrier, causing cracks to appear in the protective light.

"We're losing control!" Aslam shouted, panic creeping into his voice.

"No, we can do this!" Rafiqul responded, his voice trembling but filled with determination. "We have to push harder!"

Chapter 20: The Shikorer's Legacy

Rafiqul's mind raced as he fought to keep the ritual intact. The serpent's relentless attacks were wearing down the barrier, and Kaal-Nishachor seemed to grow stronger with each passing moment. Then, a thought crossed his mind—a desperate gamble that could either save them or doom them all.

The *Chronicle of the Shikorer* had mentioned a final, untested technique called *Shikorer-Nihoj,* a self-sacrificial spell that fused the sorcerer's life force with the binding magic, greatly amplifying its power but at a terrible cost. It was said that this spell was only used as a last resort by the Shikorer, and those who invoked it had never returned.

Rafiqul hesitated, glancing at Aslam and then at Aranyan. He could feel the guardian's gaze on him, as if the tiger understood his thoughts.

"Don't even think about it!" Aslam yelled, noticing the look on Rafiqul's face. "There has to be another way!"

"There isn't," Rafiqul replied, his voice calm and resolute. "If I don't do this, Kaal-Nishachor will break free, and we'll lose everything. I can't let that happen."

Aslam's eyes widened with horror. "No, Rafiqul! You don't have to sacrifice yourself—"

But before he could finish, Rafiqul had already begun the chant for *Shikorer-Nihoj*. He closed his eyes, feeling the energy drain from his body as it flowed into the Dhrubo-Shikor. His spirit fused with the magic of the binding spell, transforming the barrier into a radiant cocoon that engulfed Kaal-Nishachor completely.

The dark spirit howled in fury, thrashing against the binding light. "You think you can sacrifice yourself and defeat me?" it sneered. "The darkness cannot be bound by one weak boy!"

Rafiqul's vision blurred as the last of his strength faded, but just before he lost consciousness, he heard Aranyan's voice echo in his mind. "You are not alone, Rafiqul."

In that moment, a surge of power flowed into him. It was not just his magic, but the combined strength of the Shikorer's legacy, the forest's spirit, and Aranyan's own life force. The light from the Dhrubo-Shikor intensified, flooding the grove with an overwhelming brilliance that pierced through Kaal-Nishachor's dark form. The shadows screamed as they dissolved into nothingness.

The serpent's massive body began to unravel, fading into wisps of black smoke. The red eyes dimmed, and the cold voice was reduced to a faint whisper. Kaal-Nishachor's final words drifted through the air, "This is not the end..."

With a final pulse, the Dhrubo-Shikor completed the binding. The dark spirit was sealed away once and for all, trapped within the magical artifact. The light faded, and silence returned to the grove.

Chapter 21: The Cost of Victory

Rafiqul collapsed to the ground, his body exhausted and his spirit drained. Aslam rushed to his side, his face wet with tears. "Rafiqul! Please, wake up!" he cried, shaking his friend desperately.

Aranyan, too, lay still, its silver fur dimmed. The guardian tiger's eyes were closed, its breathing faint. "He used more of his life force than he should have," the tiger whispered weakly. "But there may still be a chance to save him."

Aslam's heart pounded as he listened. "What can I do?" he asked, a mix of fear and hope in his voice.

Aranyan's voice was barely audible. "The Forest's Breath... place it on his chest... and speak the words of renewal..."

Aslam grabbed the charm, his hands shaking. He placed the Forest's Breath on Rafiqul's chest and repeated the incantation that Aranyan had taught him earlier, his voice trembling with every word.

As he finished the chant, a gentle breeze stirred in the grove, carrying with it the soft fragrance of the forest. The leaves rustled as if whispering a response, and a faint glow began to emanate from Rafiqul's body. The light grew brighter, and slowly, color returned to his face.

With a soft gasp, Rafiqul opened his eyes. "Aslam...?" he whispered, his voice weak but alive.

Aslam laughed through his tears, relief flooding over him. "You idiot! Don't you ever do that again!" he exclaimed, hugging Rafiqul tightly.

Aranyan gave a deep, rumbling sigh, as if satisfied. The guardian rose to its feet, though its movements were slow. "You have done well, young sorcerers," it said. "The darkness has been sealed, but the balance of the forest will always require vigilance."

Rafiqul struggled to sit up, still feeling drained. "Aranyan... will you stay?" he asked, looking at the tiger with gratitude.

The guardian shook its head slowly. "I must return to the heart of the forest and rest," it said. "The magic that binds me to this realm is weakening. But know this—whenever the forest calls, my spirit will be with you."

With that, Aranyan turned and faded into the mist, leaving the grove bathed in a soft, golden light.

Chapter 22: The Shadow's Residue

Months passed, and life at the Sundarbans School of Magic began to return to normal. The story of the binding ritual spread, and Rafiqul and Aslam became local legends, with students constantly seeking their advice on magical matters. Yet, beneath the surface, something felt amiss.

THE RISE OF DARKNESS

Though Kaal-Nishachor had been sealed away, Rafiqul occasionally sensed faint echoes of darkness, as if small remnants of the shadow still lingered in the world. At first, he dismissed it as paranoia—a natural reaction to the trauma of the battle. But the occurrences became more frequent: whispered voices in the night, strange symbols appearing on trees, and fleeting shadows that seemed to watch him from the corners of his eyes.

One evening, as Rafiqul wandered near the grove where the final battle had taken place, he noticed a patch of ground where no grass grew, forming a perfect circle. It was as if the earth had been scarred by the ritual. The air felt colder here, heavier, and there was a faint pulsing energy beneath the soil.

Rafiqul knelt down and pressed his hand against the barren ground. The moment his skin touched the earth, a surge of darkness shot up his arm, cold and suffocating. He stumbled back, gasping for breath as his vision dimmed.

Suddenly, a voice whispered in his mind: "Did you really think it was over?"

It was Kaal-Nishachor. Somehow, a part of the dark spirit had escaped the seal, and it was regaining strength.

Rafiqul's pulse raced as he staggered back to his feet. This was more than just a scar left by the battle—it was a gateway, a place where the boundary between the material world and the darkness had been weakened. If Kaal-Nishachor's residue remained active, there was a risk that it could reopen the path to the shadow realm.

He knew he couldn't handle this alone. It was time to seek help, but not just from the usual allies. It was time to uncover secrets buried deeper than anyone at the school had dared to dig.

Chapter 23: Secrets of the Shikorer

The next morning, Rafiqul approached Professor Nuri, who had helped guide them during the binding ritual. "Professor," he began, "I think there's more we need to know about the Shikorer and their methods of sealing darkness. Kaal-Nishachor isn't completely gone—there's still a part of it that escaped the seal."

Professor Nuri's expression darkened. "I feared this might happen," she said softly. "The binding ritual was powerful, but it was not perfect. The Shikorer had knowledge of an older, more dangerous practice—one that was meant to cleanse darkness from its very source."

Rafiqul's curiosity piqued. "Why wasn't it used against Kaal-Nishachor?"

"It was considered too dangerous," Professor Nuri explained. "This technique, known as *Shikorantor,* would not just seal the darkness—it would draw it into the sorcerer's own soul, purifying it through sheer willpower. Those who attempted it risked losing themselves to the darkness they absorbed."

"Where can we learn more about this practice?" Rafiqul asked.

"There is one place," she said after a pause. "The *Aaranyak Grimoire,* an ancient text kept in the Shikorer's hidden archives. Few know of its location, and even fewer can access its secrets. It is buried deep beneath the *Mahakal Grotto,* a cavern shrouded in mystery. It's said that the grimoire is guarded by an ancient entity that tests those who seek its knowledge."

Despite the ominous description, Rafiqul's resolve was stronger than ever. He and Aslam prepared for the journey, knowing they were about to embark on a quest that could cost them more than just their lives.

Chapter 24: Into the Mahakal Grotto

The Mahakal Grotto was located far beyond the boundaries of the known forest, deep in a part of the Sundarbans where few dared to venture. As Rafiqul and Aslam approached the entrance, they saw that the cavern's mouth resembled the open jaws of a great beast, with jagged rock formations that seemed to swallow the light.

Inside, the air was damp and cool, and the walls glowed faintly with bioluminescent moss. Strange markings, ancient runes, and symbols covered the walls, telling stories of long-forgotten sorcery. As they ventured deeper, the darkness seemed to thicken, as if the very shadows were alive.

At the heart of the grotto, they came upon a massive stone door covered in intricate carvings. In the center, a circular emblem depicted the Shikorer's symbol entwined with a coiled serpent. The serpent's eyes seemed to follow their movements.

Rafiqul touched the emblem, and as he did, the carvings began to shift. The stone door creaked open, revealing a vast chamber filled with shimmering blue light. At the center of the chamber stood a pedestal, upon which rested an old, weathered book—the *Aaranyak Grimoire.*

But as they stepped closer, a shadowy figure emerged from the light. It was not Kaal-Nishachor, but something else—an ancient guardian with the body of a man and the head of a tiger. Its eyes glowed with a deep, mystical wisdom.

"To claim the knowledge within the *Aaranyak Grimoire,* you must prove yourselves worthy," the guardian spoke, its voice deep and resonant. "This is not a test of power, but of spirit."

The guardian extended its hand, and the blue light intensified, enveloping Rafiqul and Aslam. Their surroundings shifted, and they found themselves standing in a strange, ethereal landscape where the forest appeared to be made of light and shadow. Around them, illusions of their greatest fears and deepest desires began to take form, pulling them into a test of the mind and soul.

Chapter 25: Trials of the Soul

Rafiqul's surroundings morphed into a dark version of the school grounds. The buildings were twisted and broken, and the sky above was a swirling vortex of shadows. At the center of the field, he saw a vision of himself—standing alongside Kaal-Nishachor.

The dark version of himself grinned wickedly. "You always had the potential for darkness, Rafiqul. You felt the power, didn't you? It's not too late to embrace it."

"No," Rafiqul said firmly, raising his staff. "I will never give in to the darkness."

The illusion laughed, and suddenly, tendrils of shadow wrapped around Rafiqul, pulling him down. He struggled, but his strength was fading. The fear of being consumed by darkness clawed at his mind.

Then, a voice cut through the despair. "Rafiqul, remember what we've fought for!" It was Aslam's voice, echoing across the ethereal space. "You're stronger than this!"

Rafiqul closed his eyes, focusing on the memories of his journey—of Aranyan's sacrifice, of the bonds he shared with Aslam, and the courage he found within himself. A surge of light erupted from his staff, dispelling the shadows and banishing the dark illusion.

He found himself back in the grotto, with Aslam beside him, who had also managed to overcome his own trial. The guardian nodded approvingly.

"You have passed the test," it said, stepping aside. "The *Aaranyak Grimoire* is yours to study. But beware—the secrets it holds are not easily tamed."

Chapter 26: The Forbidden Technique

Rafiqul and Aslam opened the grimoire, revealing the details of the *Shikorantor* technique. It was far more complex and dangerous than they had imagined. The process involved creating a spiritual tether between the sorcerer and the darkness, allowing for the absorption of its essence. To succeed, the sorcerer needed to have an unwavering spirit and a connection with nature strong enough to endure the immense strain.

The boys knew this would be their final chance to rid the world of Kaal-Nishachor's influence. As they studied the technique, Rafiqul could feel the weight of their decision bearing down on him. If the ritual failed, he could be lost forever.

But he had come too far to turn back now. He and Aslam began preparations for the *Shikorantor,* with a new resolve to face whatever consequences awaited them.

Chapter 27: The Ritual of Shikorantor

Rafiqul and Aslam spent days preparing for the *Shikorantor* ritual, studying every detail of the forbidden technique. They chose a night when the moon was at its fullest, believing the lunar energy would help bolster their strength. The grove, still marked by the scars of the last battle, would serve as the place where light and darkness clashed once again.

The preparations were meticulous. They created a circle of enchanted stones, inscribed with ancient runes that would help contain the darkness. At the center, the Dhrubo-Shikor rested on an altar, surrounded by charms and talismans that radiated protective magic. Aslam worked tirelessly to reinforce the wards, while Rafiqul meditated, attuning his spirit to the flow of energy within the forest.

As night fell, the forest grew silent. The air was still, and a sense of anticipation hung in the atmosphere. Rafiqul and Aslam stepped into the ritual circle, their hearts pounding with a mixture of fear and determination. This time, there would be no turning back.

Rafiqul raised his staff, and Aslam followed suit. Together, they began the incantation that would activate the *Shikorantor* technique. The air around them crackled with energy as a dim, dark mist began to swirl above the Dhrubo-Shikor. The magic they invoked reached deep into the sealed realm of Kaal-Nishachor, drawing out the remnants of its power.

The shadows that had lingered since the final battle now coalesced, taking form once more. Kaal-Nishachor's voice echoed through the night, taunting them. "You seek to cleanse what cannot be purified," it hissed. "You are merely inviting the darkness into your own soul."

But Rafiqul's will did not falter. He focused on the rhythm of the incantation, allowing the words to resonate with the magic flowing through him. As the ritual progressed, a beam of light emerged from the Dhrubo-Shikor, piercing the darkness and tethering it to Rafiqul's spirit. The shadows writhed and twisted, resisting the pull of the purification.

Suddenly, Rafiqul felt a searing pain shoot through his body, as if fire and ice coursed through his veins simultaneously. The darkness fought back, clawing at his very essence. For a moment, it seemed as though it might overwhelm him, tearing his spirit apart.

"Stay strong, Rafiqul!" Aslam's voice broke through the haze of pain. He tightened his grip on his staff and channeled his own energy into the ritual, lending his strength to Rafiqul.

With Aslam's support, Rafiqul pushed deeper into the darkness, drawing it into himself, where the real struggle would begin.

Chapter 28: A Battle Within

Rafiqul's consciousness was pulled into a strange, dreamlike realm. Here, the boundaries between the real world and the spirit world blurred, and he found himself standing in a dark void. Shadows danced around him, whispering with malevolent intent.

Kaal-Nishachor's form materialized before him—now a figure of pure darkness, its features constantly shifting and changing. "You cannot purify what lies within," it said, its voice resonating like an echo. "You only feed the shadows that dwell in your heart."

In this realm, the dark spirit was not bound by the limitations of the physical world. It lashed out, sending waves of shadow that threatened to engulf Rafiqul. But as the darkness closed in, Rafiqul remembered Aranyan's words: *You are not alone.*

He reached deep within himself, drawing upon the light he had nurtured through his journey—the courage he had found, the friendships he had forged, and the sacrifices made. That inner light surged forth, clashing against the darkness. Kaal-Nishachor recoiled, but it was not defeated.

Rafiqul's battle with the darkness intensified. Every step he took forward was met with fierce resistance. The darkness was relentless, growing heavier, but so was his determination. He thought of Aslam standing outside the circle, risking everything to help him, and he knew he could not let the darkness win.

Then, through the mist of shadows, Rafiqul saw a vision—his family, his friends, and Aranyan, all watching him with expressions of hope and belief. It was as if they were lending him their strength. He could feel their spirits bolstering his own, and for the first time, he sensed Kaal-Nishachor's fear.

"You... dare to resist?" the dark spirit snarled.

Rafiqul's voice, strong and resolute, answered. "This ends now."

He released the full force of the light within him, illuminating the void. The shadows recoiled and began to dissolve, their whispers fading into silence. Kaal-Nishachor's form fragmented, breaking apart like shards of black glass.

With a final surge of energy, Rafiqul shattered the last remnants of the darkness, and suddenly, he was pulled back into the physical world.

Chapter 29: The Light's Aftermath

Rafiqul collapsed to his knees, gasping for air as the ritual circle glowed with a warm, golden light. The once oppressive darkness that had haunted the grove was gone, replaced by a tranquil aura that spread throughout the forest. The ritual had succeeded. Kaal-Nishachor was not just sealed but entirely cleansed, its essence dissolved by the power of the *Shikorantor.*

Aslam rushed to Rafiqul's side, his face filled with relief and pride. "You did it, Rafiqul," he said, helping him to his feet. "The darkness is truly gone."

Rafiqul felt a profound sense of peace wash over him, a calm he had not known since before the first encounter with Kaal-Nishachor. Yet, there was something more—a deep connection to the forest, as if a part of its spirit now flowed through him. He could sense the life in every leaf, every breeze, every creature that dwelled within the Sundarbans.

As they walked back to the school, Rafiqul noticed the change in himself. The *Shikorantor* had not only cleansed the darkness but had also awakened a new kind of magic within him—a bond with nature's spirit that went beyond mere spells and incantations.

Chapter 30: A New Beginning

Back at the Sundarbans School of Magic, Rafiqul and Aslam were hailed not only as heroes but as protectors of the forest. Headmaster Afsaruddin, with a rare smile on his usually stern face, acknowledged their bravery and dedication. "You have gone further than any student before you," he said. "But remember, true wisdom is in knowing that the path of a sorcerer never truly ends."

As Rafiqul and Aslam resumed their studies, they found themselves with a deeper purpose. They no longer sought magic for the sake of power or recognition but to protect the balance of their world and to understand the mysteries of nature's magic. They dedicated themselves to mastering the knowledge contained within the *Aaranyak Grimoire* and to teaching others the dangers and responsibilities that came with wielding such power.

Rafiqul's newfound connection to the forest granted him unique abilities. He could sense disturbances in nature and communicate with the ancient spirits that dwelled within the trees and rivers. It was as though a part of Aranyan lived on through him, guiding his actions and reminding him of the sacred duty he had undertaken.

The Whisper of Leaves

Years later, as Rafiqul stood at the edge of the grove where his journey had begun, he felt a gentle breeze rustling through the leaves. The forest seemed to whisper its gratitude, and for a moment, he could have sworn he saw a pair of golden eyes watching him from the shadows.

Though the darkness had been vanquished, Rafiqul knew that the world would always have shadows, lurking just beyond the light. It was not his duty to banish them all, but to keep the balance, to be the guardian who stood between the world and the abyss.

And so, the legend of Rafiqul and Aslam, the young sorcerers who conquered the darkness, continued to grow, inspiring future generations to seek not just the magic of spells, but the magic of courage, friendship, and the eternal fight to protect the light.

The Sundarbans thrived, not only as a school of magic but as a sanctuary where the bond between humans and nature was celebrated. And as long as there were those who remembered the lessons learned and the sacrifices made, the forest would remain a place of wonder and light, where even the whispers of shadows held no fear.

As life resumed in the Sundarbans, Rafiqul and his friends continued their work, teaching the next generation of sorcerers the importance of vigilance and respect for nature. The forest flourished, and the spirits thrived, their bonds stronger than ever.

Yet, one evening, as Rafiqul stood beneath the *Bokul Tree*, he felt a familiar presence—a fleeting shadow that danced at the edge of his vision. He turned sharply, but nothing was there. A chill ran down his spine, and he couldn't shake the feeling of being watched.

“Rafiqul?” Aslam called, approaching him with concern. “Are you alright?”

“Yeah, just... I feel like we’ve only scratched the surface,” Rafiqul replied, his gaze lingering on the shadows. “We must remain vigilant. Darkness has a way of lurking in places we least expect.”

As the sun dipped below the horizon, the forest sang its evening songs, but Rafiqul couldn’t shake the feeling that their battle was far from over. The shadows might be gone for now, but the echoes of Kaal-Nishachor lingered in the depths of the forest, a reminder that they must always be ready to protect the light.

END

My name is F. N. M. Komor, but most people know me as *Sagor Sarker*. I'm from Bangladesh, a beautiful country in South Asia. Born on 01November , 1990, I have a background in Management, with both graduate and post-graduate degrees, plus an MBA in Marketing.

Writing has always been my passion, even though it's not my profession. I love reading books and exploring new ideas, and I enjoy sharing my thoughts and stories with others. Through my writing, I aim to connect with readers and bring a bit of my world to theirs.

By- Sagor Sarker

FNMKOMOR@GMAIL.COM

THE RISE OF DARKNESS

Email: fnmkomor@gmail.com

Published by: Self-Publishing

Author: Sagor Sarker

ISBN: 979-8-227-41162-4

About the Author

My name is F. N. M. Komor, but most people know me as *Sagor Sarker*. I'm from Bangladesh, a beautiful country in South Asia. Born on 01November , 1990, I have a background in Management, with both graduate and post-graduate degrees, plus an MBA in Marketing.

Writing has always been my passion, even though it's not my profession. I love reading books and exploring new ideas, and I enjoy sharing my thoughts and stories with others. Through my writing, I aim to connect with readers and bring a bit of my world to theirs.

Read more at https://www.facebook.com/sagor.sarker.334/.

www.ingramcontent.com/pod-product-compliance
Lightning Source LLC
LaVergne TN
LVHW010117170826
845678LV00012B/2448